TOM NEEDS TO GO

OTHER BOOKS ABOUT TOM AND ELLIE

Things Tom Likes
A book about sexuality and masturbation for boys and young men with autism and related conditions
ISBN 978 1 84905 522 2
eISBN 978 0 85700 933 3

What's Happening to Tom?
A book about puberty for boys and young men with autism and related conditions
ISBN 978 1 84905 523 9
eISBN 978 0 85700 934 0

Ellie Needs to Go
A book about how to use public toilets safely for girls and young women with autism and related conditions
ISBN 978 1 84905 524 6
eIBSN 978 0 85700 938 8

Things Ellie Likes
A book about sexuality for girls and young women with autism and related conditions
ISBN 978 1 84905 525 3
eIBSN 978 0 85700 936 4

What's Happening to Ellie?
A book about puberty for girls and young women with autism and related conditions
ISBN 978 1 84905 526 0
eIBSN 978 0 85700 937 1

BY THE SAME AUTHOR

Sexuality and Severe Autism
A Practical Guide for Parents, Caregivers and Health Educators
ISBN 978 1 84905 327 3
eISBN 978 0 85700 666 0

TOM NEEDS TO GO

A book about how to use public toilets safely for boys and young men with autism and related conditions

KATE E. REYNOLDS

Illustrated by Jonathon Powell

Jessica Kingsley *Publishers*
London and Philadelphia

First published in 2015
by Jessica Kingsley Publishers
73 Collier Street
London N1 9BE, UK
and
400 Market Street, Suite 400
Philadelphia, PA 19106, USA

www.jkp.com

Library of Congress Cataloging in Publication Data
Reynolds, Kate E.
  Tom needs to go: a book about how to use public toilets safely for boys and young men with autism and related conditions / Kate E. Reynolds; illustrated by Jonathon Powell.
    pages cm
  ISBN 978-1-84905-521-5 (alk. paper)
 1. Public toilets. 2. Safety education. 3. Teenage boys--Health and hygiene. 4. Youth with autism spectrum disorders--Health and hygiene. 5. Children with autism spectrum disorders--Health and hygiene. I. Powell, Jonathon, illustrator. II. Title.
  RA607.R49 2015
  363.72'9408351--dc23
                              2014015179

British Library Cataloguing in Publication Data
A CIP catalogue record for this book is available from the British Library

ISBN 978 1 84905 521 5
eISBN 978 0 85700 935 7

Printed and bound in China

For my mother,
Alexandra Jenkins McLellan Reynolds,
for her immense support and love
shown during my recent illness.

In memory of my lovely father,
Peter Falconer Reynolds,
6 December 1932 — 3 May 2014

Kate

Thanks to Geraldine Tartan for
all her love and support.

Jonathon

A NOTE FOR PARENTS AND CAREGIVERS

Tom Needs to Go is a book about safety in public toilets for boys and young men with autism or related conditions.

As parents, caregivers or health educators we may find ourselves supporting a child of the opposite gender in a situation where that child needs the toilet in a public place.

As a mother of a boy who has a severe form of autism, until recently I had not considered what behaviours were appropriate in a men's public toilet and found myself having to research the subject for this book. Teaching 'toilet etiquette' is not something we expect to have to do. Boys typically learn this information by observing others, such as their peers or fathers. Typically developing children are also more able to ask specific questions if they are uncertain.

As boys become young men it is no longer appropriate to take them into women's toilets and we all know that disabled toilets may not be open, so we are left with the dilemma of how to 'train' our growing offspring to use public lavatories.

As a boy becomes older, some fathers may be wary of demonstrating vital information, such as showing their son how he can access his penis through the opening in his underwear in order to use urinals. Yet without this knowledge our boys and young men can be vulnerable to inappropriate advances.

Equipping boys and young men with information about expectations of proper behaviour in public toilets is one plank in ensuring their safety against possible child abuse.

This is Tom. He is shopping with his mother.

Tom needs to use the lavatory.

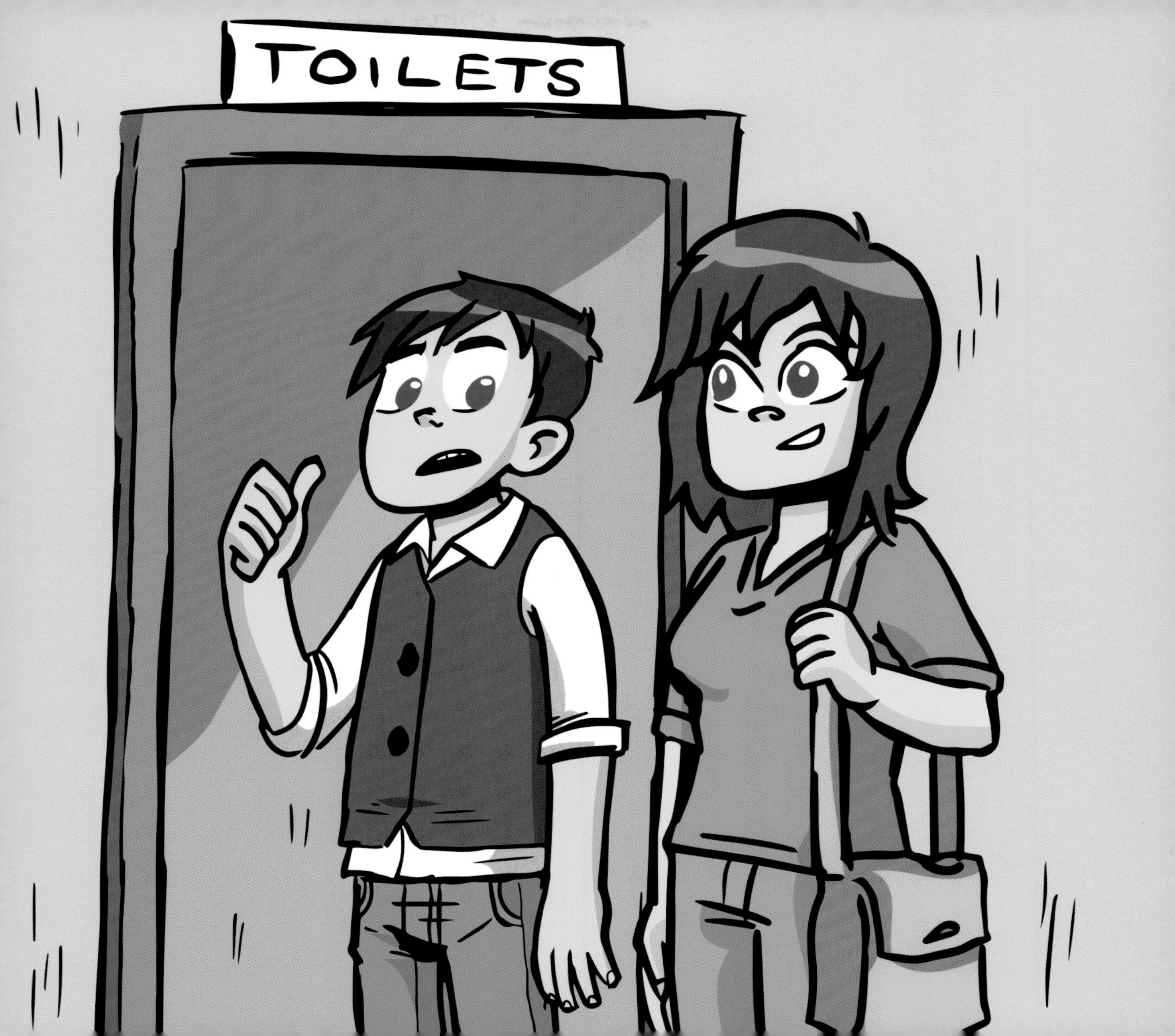
TOILETS

There are urinals and cubicles in public lavatories. Tom has to choose which to use.

Tom needs a poo so he chooses a cubicle.

Tom locks the door then pulls down his pants.

When Tom has finished pooing he wipes his bottom clean with toilet paper.

Tom pulls up his pants, flushes the lavatory then unlocks the door.

When Tom needs to pee he uses a urinal.

Tom does not stand next to or talk to anyone else, or look at anyone else's penis.

At the urinal, Tom undoes the front of his pants and pulls out his penis. Tom does not pull down his pants to pee unless he is using a cubicle and the door is locked.

Tom pees into the urinal without touching it with his penis.

When Tom has finished peeing, he shakes the pee off the end of his penis, puts his penis into his pants and does them up.

Tom always washes his hands
after a pee or a poo.

Tom joins his mother and they go shopping again. Tom wants to buy a CD!

ABOUT THE SERIES

Sexuality and sexual safety are often difficult subjects for parents, caregivers and health educators to broach with young people who have severe forms of autism and related conditions. These young people are widely perceived as being 'vulnerable', but the lack of sex education and social opportunities available only increases that vulnerability, leaving them open to child sex and other abuse. Unlike typically developing children who learn by 'osmosis' from their peers, our young people need clear and detailed information provided by those who support them.

This is one of a series of six books – three addressing issues for boys and young men and three for girls and young women. Each book tells a story about the key characters, Tom and Ellie, giving those supporting young men and women something tangible as a basis for further questions from young people. The wording is unambiguous and avoids euphemisms that may confuse readers and listeners. Many young people with severe forms of autism and related conditions are highly visual, so the illustrations are explicit and convey the entire story.

These books are designed to be read with a young person with autism, alongside other more generic reading material.